the MONSTER at the end of this book

written by **Jon Stone**
illustrated by **Mike Smollin**
featuring Grover, a **Jim Henson Muppet**
as performed on Sesame Street by Frank Oz

A SESAME STREET BOOK

Published by Western Publishing Company, Inc.
in conjunction with Children's Television Workshop.

H I J K

Library of Congress Cataloging in Publication Data

Stone, Jon.
The monster at the end of this book.
(A Little golden book)
"A Sesame Sfreet book."
SUMMARY: Grover worries page by page about meeting the monster at the end of this book.
[1. Monsters—Fiction] I. Smollin, Mike. II. Sesame Street. III. Title.
PZ7.S87785Mo [E] 77-1695
ISBN 0-307-10506-7

WHAT DID THAT SAY?

On the first page, what did that say? Did that say there will be a Monster at the end of this book???

IT DID?
Oh, I am so scared of Monsters!!!

SHH

Listen, I have an idea.
If you do not turn any pages, we will never get to the end of this book.

And that is good, because there is a Monster at the end of this book.

So please do not turn the page.

YOU TURNED THE PAGE!

Maybe you do not understand. You see, turning pages will bring us to the end of this book, and there is a Monster at the end of this book...

...but **this** will stop you from turning pages. See? I am tying the pages together so you cannot....

YOU TURNED ANOTHER PAGE!
You do not know what you are doing to me!
now...
STOP TURNING PAGES!

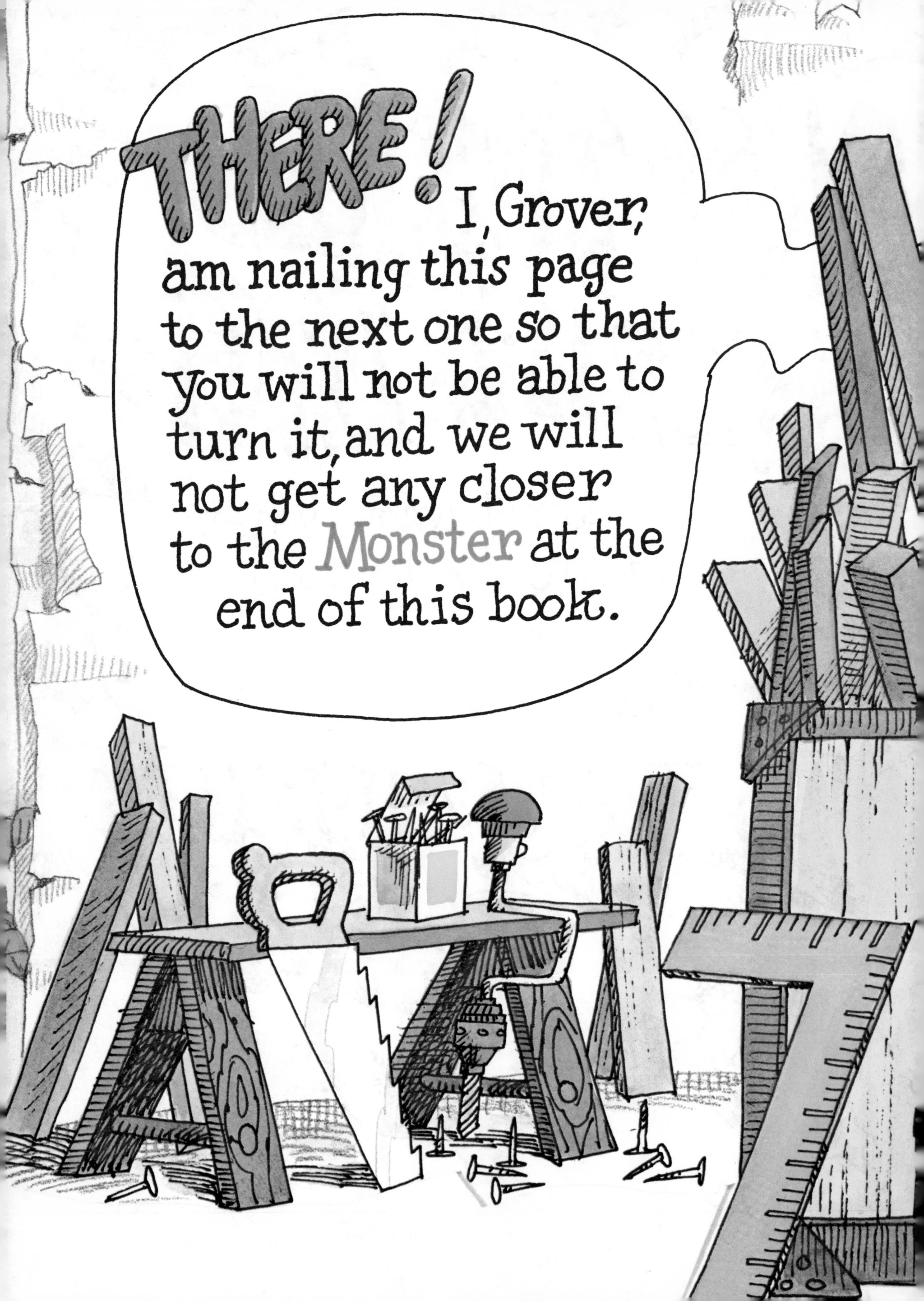
THERE! I, Grover, am nailing this page to the next one so that you will not be able to turn it, and we will not get any closer to the Monster at the end of this book.

BONK
BAM
BING!
KLONK
BONK
BING
WOOD

ALL RIGHT!
ALL RIGHT!
ALL RIGHT!
Do you know that every time you turn another page . . . you not only get us closer to the MONSTER at the end of this book, but you make
a terrible mess!

This will stop you from turning pages. A heavy, thick, solid, strong brick wall. I would just like to see you TRY to turn this page.

GLUE

Do you know that you are very strong?

The next page is the end of this book, and there is a MONSTER at the end of this book.
Oh, I am so SCARED!

PLEASE
PLEASE
do not turn the page
PLEASE
PLEASE
PLEASE

Well, look at that! This is the end of the book, and the only one here is . . .
ME
I, lovable, furry old GROVER, am the Monster at the end of this book.
And you were so SCARED!

THE
EN
I told you and told you there was nothing to be afraid of.

Oh, I am so embarrassed....